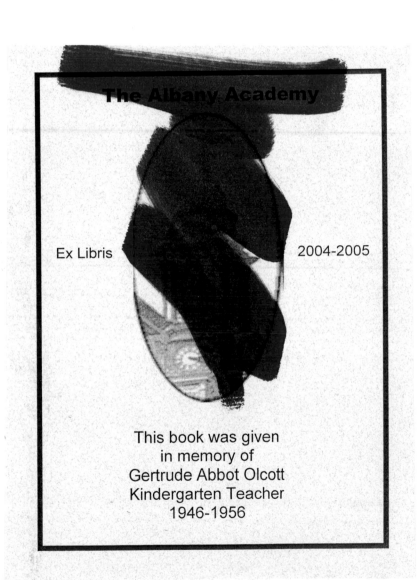

Joshua
the Giant Frog

Joshua
the Giant Frog

By Peggy Thomas
Illustrated by Cat Bowman Smith

PELICAN PUBLISHING COMPANY
Gretna 2005

For Francis, Katie, and Danny

The word "Pelican" and the depiction of a pelican are trademarks of Pelican Publishing Company, Inc., and are registered in the U.S. Patent and Trademark Office.

Library of Congress Cataloging-in-Publication Data

Thomas, Peggy.
  Joshua the giant frog / by Peggy Thomas; illustrated by Cat Bowman Smith.
      p. cm.
  Summary: Although Joshua, a giant frog, causes earthquakes when he hops and topples trees when he croaks, he can also haul a string of barges down the Erie Canal.
  ISBN 9781589802674 (hardcover: alk. paper)
  [1. Frogs—Fiction. 2. Erie Canal (N.Y.)—Fiction. 3. New York (State)—History—19th century—Fiction. 4. Tall tales.] I. Smith, Cat Bowman, ill. II. Title.

PZ7.T369273Jo 2005
[Fic]—dc22

2004017546

Printed in Singapore

Published by Pelican Publishing Company, Inc.
1000 Burmaster Street, Gretna, Louisiana 70053

Joshua the Giant Frog

From the moment the first boat floated down the Erie Canal, people living along its banks have told strange stories. It was as if mixing the waters of the Hudson and the Erie made mysterious things happen.

Red McCarthy was no bigger
than a minnow when he first heard the
tales of the bass that towed a barge, and the pike
that jumped as high as a seagull could fly. But he still
couldn't believe his eyes that day at the foot of James Street
when he scooped Joshua out of the waters of the Erie Canal.

Red went to the canal to get bait for fishing. He dipped his bucket
in and when he pulled it up, there swirling in the murky water was
the biggest polliwog Red had ever seen. It was bigger than his fist!

Red trotted home with his prize swinging at his side. He jumped up and over the pasture fence and crawled down and under the sumac trees. He was dashing around Empeyville Pond when he heard *splish, splash, sploosh.*

The polliwog had leapt from the bucket into the pond, and swam out of sight.

Every week, Red sat by the pond and watched his polliwog grow. It grew bigger than a catfish. Then it turned into a tadpole the size of a wheelbarrow. As its tail shrank, its hind legs stretched until they were longer than a packet boat. Its hide was as green as moss. Red named it Joshua.

Bugs didn't come big enough for Joshua, so he took to eating chipmunks and squirrels. Red rescued his dog Ruby more than once when she sniffed too close to the water's edge.

When Joshua jumped, the earth shook. Scientists came from all around the world to study the strange earthquakes that jostled the little town.

If Joshua was in a hurry, he could cross two counties in a single leap. But he wasn't careful about where he landed. Rolph Rhinehart had to repair his outhouse four times.

Every time Joshua hopped back in the pond, he sent up a spray of water fifty feet into the air—basements flooded and gardens drowned.

Joshua's deep *garrumph, garrumph* puffed his throat out with such force that he knocked down all the trees around the pond. The booming bass rattled every window. It cracked Old Lady Lindsey's teacups, and toppled the oldest church steeple.

When Joshua sang into the night, no one slept.

Finally, the people of Empeyville held a town meeting.

"What are we going to do?" Farmer Anderson
yawned. "I'm so tired, I almost plucked the cow and
milked the chicken."

Another farmer shouted, "At least you've got milk.
My cows up by the pond are too nervous to give."

"Well, my pony is too scared to go down Old Pond Road," said the preacher.

Old Lady Lindsey waved her cane and said, "My cats are missing."

Everyone agreed that Joshua had to go.

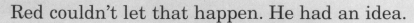

Red couldn't let that happen. He had an idea.

That summer it was drier than chalk and the canal was nothing more than a wet rag lying across the state. A line of barges was stranded between Rome and Syracuse. Canalers had hitched up one hundred mules, then two hundred oxen, but nothing could budge the boats.

From the back of the hall, Red shouted, "I bet Joshua could move those barges."

Children giggled, and the men in the first row crossed their arms and shook their heads. "It'll never work," they grumbled.

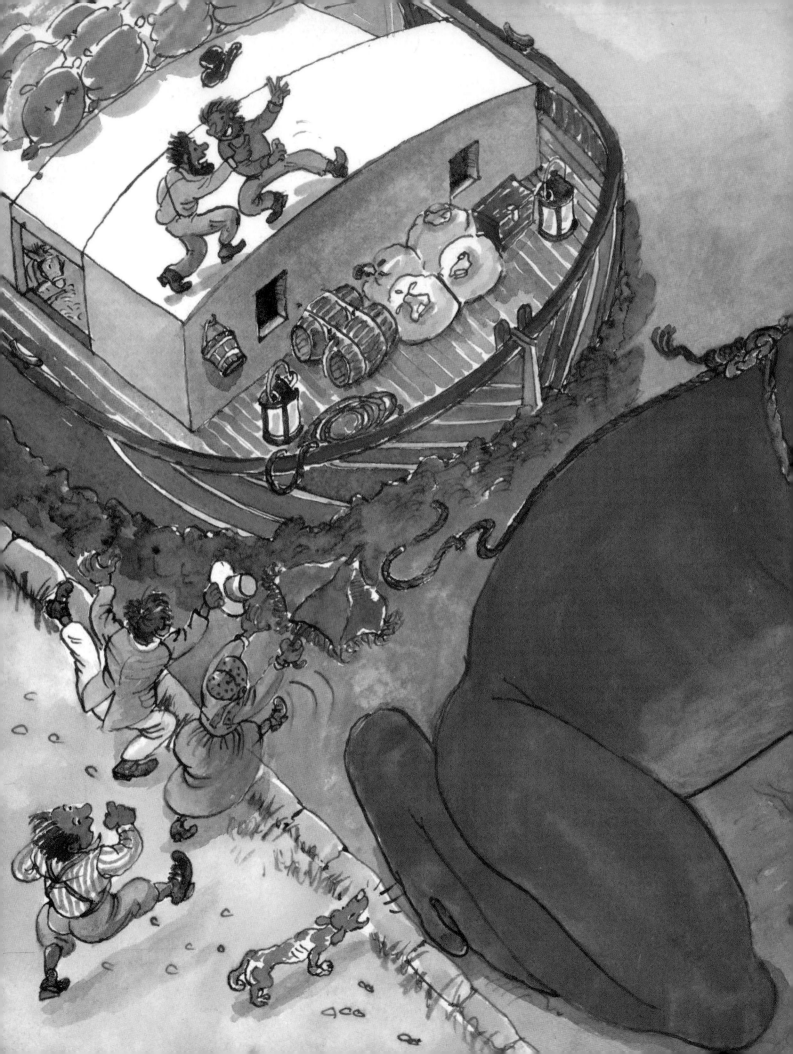

But the next day, Joshua hauled the boats all the way to Albany. The governor personally thanked Joshua for deepening the Erie Canal.

After that, the saddle-smith fashioned a special harness to fit Joshua's bulky body, and the women held a quilting bee and stitched his name on it.

Joshua hauled lumber too heavy for horses, and pulled tree stumps for farmers. Each job was bigger than the last—a four-foot stump, a five-foot stump, a rock the size of a buggy, or a boulder the size of a barn.

Then after a hot day of work when Joshua hopped
back in his pond, the children would cool off in his
spray. At night Joshua's showers reflected in the moon-
light, and when the sky was clear, the shimmering
lights could be seen as far away as Alaska.

At the end of each day, Joshua would sing his evening song. The folks from Westdale still complained that his deep *garrumph* rattled the windows, but the people of Empeyville enjoyed his thunder. And on the Fourth of July, he played the *oom-pa-pa* part for the band.

Years went by, and Joshua and Red grew older. Joshua's glossy green hide faded to gray, and Red's flaming hair lightened to white. Red was now the mayor of Empeyville and held his own town meetings.

"Joshua," Red said one day. "We need you to straighten out the dangerous curves on Snake Hill Road." It was an impossible job, but if anyone could do it, Joshua could.

The very next morning, Joshua sat with his well-worn harness at the end of Snake Hill Road where it forked into James Street. A man from the railroad pounded an iron stake deep into the pavement. Twelve men carried the chain and attached it to Joshua's harness.

As the sun rose, the crowd gathered.

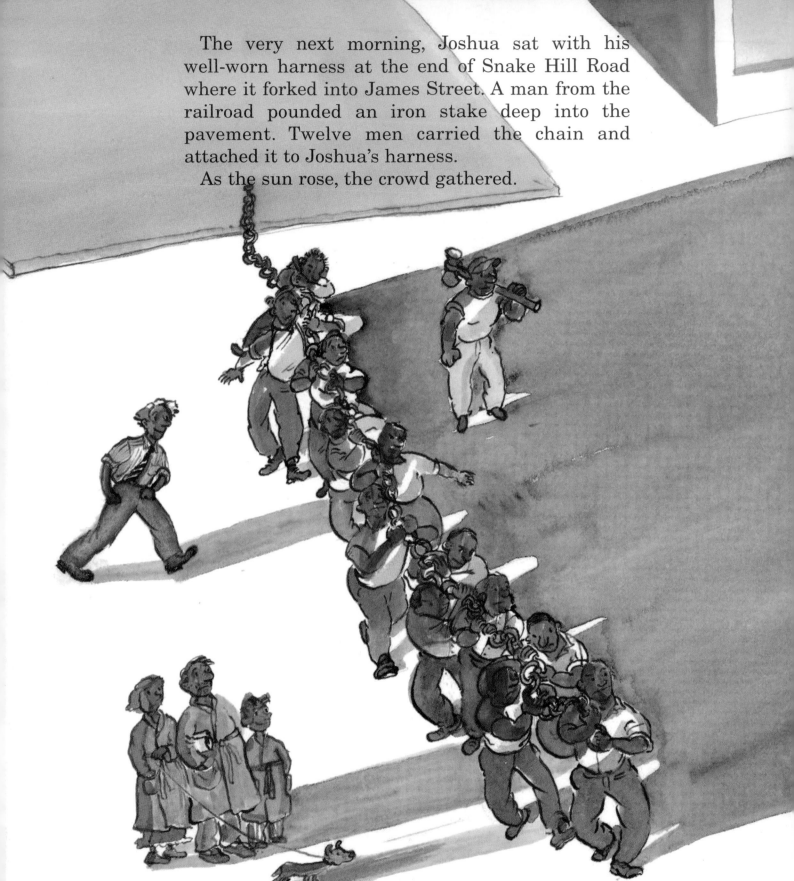

Joshua flexed his iron thighs. The townspeople held their breath. Then with one mighty leap Joshua the Giant Frog flew into the air. The chain snapped taut. The road lifted like a ribbon. When it floated back to earth it lay straight as an arrow and flat as canal water.

To this day, Snake Hill Road crosses James Street
and continues on for six more miles. The people of
Empeyville called it his greatest feat, but old Red
knew that Joshua had other things on his mind.

Sailors say that Joshua is the foghorn heard in the mist of the St. Lawrence. People in Detroit tell of a mysterious moving island on Lake Michigan. Some say he went south to Panama to deepen another canal. But Red's great-grandson says that on hot summer nights his windows rattle, and he can hear a deep *garrumph, garrumph* coming from the waters of the Erie Canal.

DATE			